ANOINTED
FOR CALLING

Discover Your Calling &
Transform The World

Third Edition

SAMUEL LEE

ANOINTED FOR CALLING

Discover Your Calling & Transform The World

Third Edition

SAMUEL LEE

FOUNDATION PRESS

ANOINTED FOR CALLING

Discover Your Calling & Transform The World

SAMUEL LEE

Published by Foundation Press
A division of Foundation University Press
Verrijn Stuartweg 31, Diemen 1112 AW, The Netherlands

www.foundationuniversitypress.com

978-94-90179-04-5

To my sons and daughter
Anthony, Joseph & Esther:

born for a purpose
made for a reason

known by the Creator
chosen by Christ

to fulfill His will
by being just who they are

≪Life is Beautiful…≫

Papa

Anointed for Calling is a book for all believers, a must read for all Christians who desire maturity. It will cause the Church to rise up and help each believer to grow into full maturity and ministry. It is a Holy Spirit-inspired, biblically-explained book about the ministry of God's people.

Anointed for Calling shows us how to look at the Kingdom of God and our ministry within it. It combines insights and revelations about the anointing, and it reveals how a person can get a yoke-breaking anointing. It will enable you to determine and practice your calling and eliminate every doubt and confusion as you progressively mature. Your calling and anointing are the maturity-building blocks that unlock your future destiny and they will help you fulfil your dream. They are the seeds to your great harvest. This is a prophetic book with pragmatic principles.

John P. Kelly
President,
Leadership Education For Apostolic
Development (LEAD)

CONTENT

INTRODUCTION

In my ministry for the past 15 years, I have met people who sincerely love God and are willing to serve the Lord Jesus Christ. But they often waste their time and energy engaging in activities they are not called to do. They are confused simply because they do not know what their calling is and for what work they are truly anointed. Imagine if all Christians would correctly know and practice their callings in their lives. How rapidly would the Kingdom of God advance and how great an impact would it produce for humanity?

Many people have the desire to work for God, but they have no idea about how to do it. Some are hanging in the air and wondering what God wants them to do. Likewise, some doubt whether they are already doing what God has anointed them to do. In this book you will be trained to look at your life in a new way. You will discover your calling and more. If you are already moving in the calling God has given you, this calling will be reshaped, polished, and sharpened. God is not looking at our weaknesses. He is looking at what He can make out of us within the framework of our abilities and beyond.

Knowing our calling in life parallels the anointing we receive from the Lord. Understanding the anointing will help the body of Christ be more effective for the Kingdom of God. Therefore, this book will help you understand the anointing, including what it means and how it relates to your calling. Before reading this book, you need to know that you are created for a purpose and a reason. You have to remember this: **"There is no unemployment in the Kingdom of God!"**

Part I

Preparations

REFORMATIONS & DEFINITIONS

The twenty-first century is the most exciting period in history to be alive. Since the birth of Jesus Christ until today, humanity has experienced enormous degrees of transformations. What was impossible to accomplish a thousand years ago became possible hundreds of years ago. Likewise, what was not possible a hundred years ago is now possible today. Thanks to breakthroughs in science and technology our current world is changing faster than we ever could have imagined. Three decades ago, Internet technology was beyond our reach, but now we are empowered with access to all the information superhighways in the world. In a fraction of a second, we can send or receive a letter. Plus, technology has opened up so many more options.

Let's pursue this idea further. Since 2000 years ago until today, what role did the Church play in the history of humanity? Where does the Church stand in the middle of all these technological and human advancements? In the past two millennia, the Church greatly contributed to the formation and direction of history. Not all her contributions, however, were positive for there were numerous wars, crimes and barbaric acts that took place in the name of the Church and God.

From the time the Church was born, Christianity has had its revivals and downfalls. During the Middle Ages, the Roman Catholic Church gradually lost her power and the world witnessed the birth of the Protestant movement in the early 1500s. This influenced the course of history in Western Europe and eventually the entire world. After a few centuries, however, the Protestant churches also lost their fire and enthusiasm. Some of them became as traditional and conservative as the Catholic Church. As a result of this regression, different movements were born. In the 1700s and 1800s, various revivals impacted Europe, and their results spread to the rest of the world. In a similar way the 1900s experienced various revivals. For example, the Pentecostal revival impacted society. It dealt with racial issues and the severe discrimination in America that occurred between the white and the black churches. The Pentecostal movement also provided a modest starting point for more freedom among women in the Church.

After World War II, the traditional Church in Western Europe and the United States declined while

Pentecostal/Charismatic churches and many forms of Born Again Christianity grew rapidly, especially in developing countries. Many traditional churches closed down and their buildings were used for secular purposes. Many became museums, company compounds, and even discotheques and casinos. Today, a century later, with technology and multimedia booming, Christianity is gaining a new dimension. This chapter will examine certain issues and explains terms such as "Christianity," "Church," "ministry," "work," and "evangelism."

If we truly want to reach the world with the Gospel and be used by God as effectively as possible, then it is time for us to put aside the old wineskin and start using new wine in the new wineskin. To do so, we need to redefine and reform our ideals.

Christianity

Unfortunately, our understanding of Christianity is based upon wrong concepts. Many people with whom I interact say they are Christians because they go to church on Sundays, observe Easter, and exchange gifts on Christmas. However, going to a gathering or following a tradition proves nothing about someone's faith. Many others call themselves Christians because they were born into a Christian home or society. Their parents or grandparents are Christians and, therefore, they think they automatically assume the same faith. Again, these situations do not make a person a Christian. We have to realize that we must be born again, grow in the spirit, and be an active part of the Father's Kingdom. Further, many people stop at being born again; they don't go deeper than the "born-again experience" and they disregard the call to follow Jesus.

Christianity is not a title; it is a way of life through the Holy Spirit. Christianity means doing what God asks you to do. A born again Christian is a person who does the will of the Father here on earth. Christianity is neither measured by the frequency of our church attendance nor the length of our prayers or fasting. These are not *the* standards of faith. Christianity is not measured by our deeds; it is evidenced by when the Word of God becomes flesh in our lives. Therefore, a Christian is someone who is born again and partakes in the Kingdom of God. A Christian is someone who lives according to the Word and Spirit. Based on this, a Christian is someone who makes a difference here on earth for the Kingdom of God. And this difference doesn't have to be big!

Lastly, a Christian must be deeply convinced that the only unique solution for this dying world is Jesus Christ. His love message must flow from us to our families, and then to our society, and then to our world. However, some Christians live a dual life. They believe wholeheartedly in the Lord, but they keep their faith to themselves. They live according to what society dictates. They cannot join their faith and the Bible with their daily activities. This gap causes them to compromise. From one side, they try to be good people and believe in Jesus for salvation and life eternal, but on the other hand, they do not believe that the Kingdom message of the Gospel is able to influence every aspect of their lives, the society, and the entire world. Unfortunately, there are many Christians who have similar beliefs. For this reason, much of the arts, sports, politics, economy, and science are being dominated by men and women who do not know Christ and are not willing to give the Gospel a chance. No wonder the young and the old alike watch MTV and the Hollywood films. Environmentalists come from the New Age and not the Church. All of this happens because the majority of Christians are so busy with religious activities within the four walls of our holy church buildings.

True Christians must have faith in action! They must have faith in their faith! Act by faith! They must believe that the Gospel of Jesus Christ offers the answers for every aspect of life on this earth. We have to believe that we can make the best music and the best movies. We need to be the owners of successful businesses. We need to be the best lawyers, doctors, politicians, economists, and presidents. We have to believe that Jesus is the answer for the various ills in the world such as terrorism, hunger, AIDS, poverty, same-sex marriages, abortion, and the many other social and political issues. We have to touch the natural with the super-natural. How? The secret is found in bridging the gap between *knowing our calling* and *putting it in practice*!

Church

Another important term we need to understand is "Church." We have to realize we are the Church! We need to know that the Church is not limited to an organization, denomination, or a bureaucratic institution confined in a building with offices, chairs, and worship rooms that follow fixed times of worship and days of gathering. The Church is the place where two or more people are gathered together in Jesus' Name; this can be anywhere — in the house, in the work-place, at school, or in the street!

Two thousand years ago the Church of Jesus Christ was born in the street corners and market-places of Jerusalem, Judea, Samaria, and the ends of the world. The Church was neither born under any religious system nor was it confined to a synagogue! The Church was born out of people and the Holy Spirit together with the demonstration of His power. The early Church was not built out of bricks and walls; it was made of people who had a message of life, hope, power, and victory! The Christ-born Church was indeed so powerful that the contemporary superpowers bowed to the Kingdom message of the Gospel. From Jerusalem to Rome, from India to

Spain, from Egypt to Ethiopia and Persia, these nations were impacted through the Gospel. Although this Church of flesh and blood was opposed, burnt alive, fed to lions, crucified upside down, raped, and cut into pieces, no one could stop the Church from surviving and flourishing.

First, the Pentecostal Church was not an organization born in cathedrals and chapels. Instead, it is a living organism, formed in the marketplaces, where ordinary believers with extraordinary faith practice their callings in life. The Marketplace — this is where we can practice our calling; this is where the Church must be!

Second, the Church is not a building. Many people think a Church is a place where people can gather once a week for a few hours to pray and hear messages. But the Church is more than that. It consists of people. The Church is the gathering of God's people. It's not just a building with pictures of the cross or stained windows and wooden pews!

We must realize the Church is a Kingdom — God's Kingdom here on earth! The Church is God's embassy on earth. Christ is the King. The Church is His government. And we are His ambassadors, representing Him on this earth (2 Corinthians 5:20). If we continue to believe that the Church is a building, we will not impact the world! The Church exists wherever we represent Jesus Christ to be the Supreme Lord over every situation and everything. It starts at home with the family and extends toward our communities and beyond. When we realize that we are the Church everyday and every moment of our lives, then many things will start to change. Something better will happen to the world. We will be able to influence our world with power and impact it through the authority of Christ!

The Church exists so that the Father's will can be done here on earth. Remember what Jesus said: *"For where two or three come together in my name, there am I with them"* (Matthew 18:20). Unfortunately, we hide ourselves from the world and limit our Christian lives around the four walls of our buildings, and we keep our God-given authority and talents for ourselves.

The current universal Church needs to be changed; she has to participate proactively in blessing the society and manifesting Christ's power in every facet of human life. Modern man is not interested in goose-bumps and golden dust manifestations, falling on the floor and rolling on the altar for hours. The world wants to see our lives changed. The world wants to read our lives, not our sermons!

Some of the brethren have turned the Church into a circus of religious activities. God, though, wants souls being saved, trained, and mobilized. He wants the Gospel preached everywhere and by every means. God wants to see His people making a difference and impacting humanity in radical and loving ways. He wants the Church to start using the arts, music, movies, science, politics, economics, commerce and other disciplines to bless the lives of people in the Name of her Bridegroom and King — Jesus Christ. But how can we do this if we have a wrong understanding of the Church?

Third, the Church is a Kingdom without boundaries. It has no geographical limitations. To illustrate, United Kingdom is United Kingdom within her legal geographical boundaries. So is America, Canada, Iran, Korea or any other country! The Kingdom of God, however, is not the same! This Kingdom has no borders. God's Kingdom is everywhere and anywhere! This Kingdom is present wherever and whenever believers are together in Jesus' Name! This can be in India, Mozambique, Argentina, or China. This Kingdom can even be in the most hostile countries and nations. Because of this, nobody is able to stop this Kingdom or attack it, because this Kingdom is within the devil's territory destroying it from the heart and root. We have invaded the ground already and the Kingdom will continue growing!

In Daniel 2:24–45, the Prophet Daniel interpreted a particular dream of King Nebuchadnezzar of Babylon. The interpretation was that one day Babylon would fall and there would be three kingdoms to follow it. Most importantly, a kingdom would eventually come that would never be destroyed:

"In the time of those Kings, the God of heaven will set up a kingdom that will never be destroyed, nor

> *will it be left to another people. It will crush all those kingdoms and bring them to an end, but it will itself endure for ever. This is the meaning of the vision of the rock cut out of mountain not by human hands"* (Daniel 2:44).

Throughout the generations, Daniel's interpretation became true. Three important kingdoms followed Nebuchadnezzar's kingdom. They were the Persian kingdom (now Iran), the Greek Empire, and the Roman Empire (now Italy). During the Roman Empire, a Messiah was born unto us. In the interpretation of Daniel, Jesus Christ symbolized the rock that fell on the feet of the Roman Empire, and within the span of 300 years the Roman Empire bowed to the message of the Gospel. Since then, no one could stop this Kingdom. Many tried to conquer it, kill its citizens, and ban its King. But today, this Kingdom grows faster than ever before. It all started 2000 years ago according to the interpretation of Daniel the prophet!

The Kingdom of God

How does this Kingdom function? This Kingdom is ruled by Jesus Christ, the King of Kings. He is seated at the right hand of the Father and He rules the heavens and the earth! After Him is the Holy Spirit who brings the will of God and the message of Christ to the contemporary Church. The Holy Spirit is the Prime Minister of this Kingdom. He is the Leader and Guide of the Church. While Jesus is seated at the right hand of the Father, the Holy Spirit is present here on earth. He makes sure that Christ's salvation is known and done by the Church here on earth! Jesus Christ is King. The Holy Spirit is the Prime Minister. And the angels are His servants. Together, these three form the invisible government. Beside this comes the visible government of God which consists of apostles, prophets, evangelists, pastors and teachers. In addition, there is God's people or God's nation:

> *"It was he who gave some to be <u>apostles</u> (1), some to <u>be prophets</u> (2), some to be <u>evangelists</u> (3), some to be <u>pastors</u> (4) and <u>teachers</u> (5), to prepare <u>God's</u> <u>people</u> (6) for **works of service**, so that the body of Christ may be built up until we all reach unity in faith and knowledge of the son of God and become mature, attaining to the whole measure of the fullness of Christ"* (Ephesians 4:11–13, emphases added).

Basically, we call this the "five-fold ministry." However, I would like to bring additional teaching to this interpretation. I call the above "the six-fold ministry" because besides the five ministers — the apostles, prophets, evangelists, pastors and teachers — there is another ministry mentioned in this passage. It is the ministry of God's people. The words "to *prepare God's people for works of service"* means to prepare the believers — the Kingdom-citizens — for ministry. The word "service" is the same as the word "ministry." Thus, everybody in the Kingdom is a minister, a servant, and a person who gives service in order for the Kingdom of God to advance through maturity and unity worldwide! This means that everyone who calls himself a true Christian already has a ministry and has his or her own place in the Kingdom. What then is the specific description of this ministry since the other five ministries have a clear job description?

The Ministry of God's People (MGP) is somehow different; it can cover every rank and facet of activity. MGP offers a large field of possibilities. Imagine if everyone were apostles, prophets, evangelists, pastors and teachers. What would happen? We would be preaching, teaching and playing apostle to each other while the world was perishing!

The MGP contains endless fields of work in God's Kingdom. This is what Jesus referred to when He said, *"The work is plenty but the workers are few."* You don't have to leave your jobs and enter so-called "full-time ministry" to serve the Lord. You can be a minister in the field of your work, talent, or any other thing. You can be a taxi driver and serve the Lord. You can be a lawyer. You can be a mother. If we understood this fact more deeply, we would impact our world more rapidly and stronger than ever before. Many people mistakenly feel guilty about what they were doing in the world before they were saved. Some quit their jobs to enter a theological seminary and become a pulpit minister. From the other side, however, unbelievers take their places in the working field and start advancing their talents and pursuing creativity in their fields. When this happens, Christians surrender their territories to the enemy. Now we are crying about why the world is the way it is!

For too long we have been fooling ourselves into thinking that only the clergymen or the pulpit ministers are supposed to do the works of God. We have considered our pastors, our Sunday school teachers, and our city evangelists as "the" men of God. In reality, though, the men and women in the ministry of God's people are just as important and vital as the ones in the five-fold ministry!

Today, there are many spiritually-fat Christians. They eat spiritual food on Sundays to gain head knowledge, but they fail to exercise what they have learned because they think they are second class citizens in the Kingdom!

As you read this book remember what Jesus said, *"There are many works, but the workers are few."* You and I need to realize that even if all the so-called clergy of the world were united, there would still be plenty of work remaining. For God's work to be done, God's people must be involved. In the Kingdom of

God, there should be no unemployment because there is work for everyone. Be ready because God wants to use you! He wants to make you fly higher, aim bigger, and use you in the sweetness of your dreams. He wants to touch the essence of your being. Get ready to fly for Jesus!

2

THINGS YOU NEED TO KNOW

The Lord said, *"My people suffer for they lack knowledge"* (Hosea 4:6). There are essential points you must know so you can function properly in your calling. They are: 1. Everyone (including you) has a place in God's Kingdom. 2. You are needed more than ever in the Kingdom. You are important.

Realize: You Have a Place

From the moment you became a born again Christian, God already prepared a certain place for you in His Kingdom: "Before I was born the LORD called me; from my birth he has made mention of my name" (Isaiah 49:1). God had a plan for you when He formed you in your mother's womb. However, due to our free will, God never forces His plan upon us! He may show us our place in the Kingdom, but He never forces us to fill up that place. Everything depends on our choices and whether we are willing to fill that missing part in the Kingdom or not. If you call yourself a Christian but you feel you have no place in the Kingdom, you are wrong! You have a place; only you can take that place when you surrender to the Lord and agree with His plans for your life.

Confess: You Are Needed

You also have to realize that you are extremely important and needed. You need to feel as if the world would not turn if you were not here! You are wanted! You are called! You are needed more than ever before! Many think the opposite. They feel they are insignificant for society and the Kingdom of God. Jesus is desperate; the workers for the harvest are few.

Day and night we are in a constant spiritual battle. In this war everybody is needed. Whether you are a man, woman, child, or old or young, you are needed. *You are needed!* The world is dying and it cries in agony and death. In a world where evil reigns, we need to realize how important we are. We are the salt of the world and we are the light of hope. We are the ambassadors of the Kingdom, the peacemakers and life-changers through the Gospel. We have to restlessly work to advance the Kingdom of the Lord, our Father's Kingdom.

If companies like Toyota, Coca Cola, Samsung, General Motors and many others can use everyone and everything to reach the world with their products, how much more should we labor for the Gospel? You can find the products of these companies in every village and town, and even in the most remote areas. Yet 2000 years have passed and not everyone has heard the name of Jesus and the testimony of His death and resurrection, and His life-changing Gospel. Why? Because while we are sleeping and wondering about our purpose in life, the people in these companies are up all night planning and strategizing about how to take their materialistic products to the world! Why aren't we?

Start confessing that you are important and needed in the Kingdom of God. Change your negative attitudes. The Father wants to hear from your lips about your readiness. He wants you to confess that you are working for Him.

Pray for Direction

After realizing your place and confessing your importance, you have to pray! Without prayer you will never be able to know your calling or maintain your calling in life. Pray with an open mind; let the Spirit of God talk to your soul.

Through prayer, you will passionately understand what the Lord wants from you. Praying regularly will enable you to receive visions and directions for your calling.

Fellowship with the Spirit

An hour of prayer everyday doesn't mean fellowship-ping with the Holy Spirit! We have to go far beyond a simple prayer life! Our fellowship should be 24 hours a day. Your spiritual radar must be connected day and night. This gives you access to new visions and strategies and it will help you find the right tools in fulfilling your calling. There are inspirations and revelations you get when you are connected to the 'Spirit wide-web' of the throne room of God.

Jesus spoke of the Holy Spirit to His disciples:

> *"If you love me, you will obey what I command. And I will ask the Father, and he will give you another Counselor to be with you forever — the Spirit of truth"* (John 14:16–17).

> *"All this I have spoken while I am still with you. But the Counselor, the Holy Spirit, whom the Father will send in my name, will teach you all things and will remind you of everything I have said to you"* (John 14:25–26).

The Holy Spirit is the Spirit of all truth, the truth about all things, including you and everything that concerns you. He knows the solution for everything you need or want. He knows the best way to take for your life journeys. The only thing you need to do is connect with Him. Ask Him. Talk to Him. He who is the Spirit of Truth will help you. He will speak right into your heart. He will whisper into your ear and tell you what you need to do to fulfill your calling. For example, He will show you what kinds of strategies you will need. He will give you the proper tools and empower you.

Here's an example. Years ago, my wife started her own beauty salon in one of the prestigious hotels in Amsterdam. At that same time, we started a ministry in a small building. Our vision was that through our beauty salon we would be able to support the ministry and cover our expenses. However, things were not as easy as we thought! My wife worked very hard in the salon and I worked 24 hours a day for the service of God and people.

We often received midnight calls asking us to pray for the sick, settle disputes, or counsel people. We went to sleep late at night, we woke up early, and we worked very hard. Aside from that, we also received dooming prophecies and messages from people who claimed that the Lord's anger was upon us because my wife was not in full time ministry with me. They said the Lord was not happy with her being the owner of a beauty salon. At first, I agreed with them and repented. I tried to stop my wife from working even though I knew that was what she was supposed to do. However, deep within me I knew that these comments were not true. I knew my wife's heart, and I knew that she loved what she did. I also knew her talents and I was certain that she was not a pulpit minister. Instead, she is more of a marketplace minister who supports me and shares my vision to advance the Kingdom.

I still remember the days when we didn't have enough clients in the salon and the little money we earned went directly to paying the rent of the salon and church expenses. We experienced days when there was no food on our table, and the little we had was given to us by the church and ministry. A few years passed and we saw improvement, although not as much we liked. In the meantime, my wife and I prayed day and night and we asked God for wisdom until one day it became *Rhema* to us that the Spirit of God is the Spirit of *all* truth. Therefore, He is able to teach us many things about how to make the business grow. We realized that the Lord created people and their hair. He knows the needs people have with their hair. So we prayed to the Holy Spirit many times and asked Him for advice. We asked Him to give us something that would bring us farther than any other beauty salon. Then the Holy Spirit inspired my wife and told her that there are people who have curly hair who want their hair to be straightened. The conventional method of hair straightening damages the hair and it only last for a few days, weeks, or perhaps a month. Then the curly hair returns.

The Holy Spirit, however, inspired my wife and her mother to experiment and start a new and revolutionary hair straightening system in Europe based on natural ingredients. This system makes the hair remain straight for at least three to six months. This was the birth of a product and hair treatment called WONDER-STRAIGHT. Within a year, the media focused on WonderStraight. The salon became so famous that even people from Italy and Spain would fly for 2 hours to come to Amsterdam for a hair treatment in her salon. Many Dutch celebrities became our clients and now we are moving much faster and higher than ever before. All of this happened when the Holy Spirit changed our expectations and we trusted Him to give us the best advice, the best strategy, and the best way for doing business. Now this business is blessing the ministry much more than ever before.

If you want to be effective in your calling, connect to the Spirit of all Truth, the Holy Spirit. Ask Him and He will come and help you in all things!

The Anointing

The last and most important point you need to know by heart is the anointing. Many people who search for their calling in life, or who already function in their calling, forget one important thing — the anointing. Many focus on man-made ideas and visions rather than focusing on God's specific plan and anointing for them. Therefore, I will deal with this very crucial subject in the following chapters. We will explore the word "anointing" and its relationship to our calling: *Without the anointing, we are not able to function and fulfill our calling in life!*

PART II

THE ANOINTING

3

What Is the Anointing?

The word "anointing" is one of the most popular words among Christians today. Many use this word very lightly, and many others use it in the wrong context. In my life, I have met many who are moving in God's anointing and producing good fruits. These are people who make a difference by being anointed. The good news is that you can be one of them!

You must know that it is God's will for everyone in His Kingdom to be anointed. He wants to use you, but in order to do so, He has to anoint you first. It is only with the "official anointing" of God that you can fulfill your destiny and His will for your life! Oftentimes, people speak about the anointing, and they say things like: *"Oh, I am so anointed." "I feel the anointing." "The message was anointed."* Or, *"The music was anointed."* Somehow, though, I feel that they are using this word very lightly! In this chapter, we will examine the actual meaning of the term, "anointing," and we will also learn what is *not* the anointing!

Definition of Anointing

The anointing occurs when **someone or something** *is* **set apart** *by* **the Lord Jesus Christ,** *through* **the Holy Spirit,** *to* **fulfill** *a* **special task** *for* **God's Kingdom on earth!** In the Old Testament, the word anointing is called *Maashah*, which means "to anoint, smear, or consecrate." The New Testament uses the Greek word *Aleipho*, which is used for "an anointing" of any kind of thing, whether for physical refreshment after washing or anointing a material for special use! In the New Testament, another word that is used to refer to anointing is *Chrio*. *Chrio* is used to indicate that Jesus Christ is **God's anointed one.** The word "Christ" comes from the word *Chrio*!

The best example to illustrate our definition is the life of Jesus Christ! After He was baptized by John, and after His 40 days of fasting and temptation by Satan, Jesus Christ started His official ministry! On the Sabbath day, He entered the synagogue in Nazareth and opened the scroll of the prophet Isaiah and read:

"The Spirit of God is on me, because <u>he has anointed me</u> <u>to preach</u> good news to the poor. He has sent me <u>to proclaim</u> freedom for the prisoners. And recovery of sight for the blind, <u>to release</u> the

oppressed, to proclaim the year of the Lord's favor" (Luke 4:18–19, emphases added).

These verses describe the mission and purpose of Jesus. By reading these verses carefully, we will find certain components and patterns that we can use to analyze and understand the concept of anointing.

Components of "the Anointing"

Being set apart for a purpose by the Holy Spirit

Jesus said the Spirit of God is upon Him. The Holy Spirit anointed Him (*set Him apart*) for a special purpose, namely, *to preach the good news, to set the captives free and to proclaim the year of the Lord's favor.* He was set apart for this purpose!

Anointing always has a purpose; it has a job description; it has a mission to fulfill. Many people mistake feeling good in a meeting or being filled with the Holy Spirit immediately with the anointing. However, you can be filled with the Holy Spirit and yet not be anointed for the tasks you are presently doing. In other words, whenever you feel the anointing of God come upon you, it must have a purpose and a mission. When we say the music was anointed, this means the music was set apart for a purpose. It opens heaven's gates for Gods' glory, and it brings worshippers before the throne room of God. Or when we say a message was anointed, this means the message was set apart for a specific purpose. It can be to edify, train, heal, or any other purpose God intended! A lot of shouting and emotion in a message does not necessarily mean that the message was anointed! Many people are confusing emotional feelings with the anointing. With a little manipulation of the sound system and lighting, we can easily produce an emotional atmosphere whereby people may feel a chill and thrill in their bodies. The anointing, though, does not depend upon how we feel!

Are you anointed for the things you are doing in your life? Or, are you someone who goes from one church service to another, from one revival meeting to another, and has every preacher lay his or her hands on you so that you may feel God's presence? If all these things do not change your life and do not set you apart to do God's purposes and plans, then there is something wrong with either you or the places you are going to!

What then is God's calling in your life? What is your reason for living? Is what you do for God in the name of Jesus really what He has asked you and anointed you to do? Many people fail in their Christian lives because they want to do things for God, but they were never anointed by God! They fail because they cannot discern whether God has anointed them or whether it is their own will and power that gets the job done! This is the reason why they force things on themselves but they never pro-duce fruit! If what you are doing for God under the umbrella of "the anointing" does not bring forth good fruit, then you need to ask yourself whether you are truly anointed.

Can you define your anointing like Jesus did in few words? Every person who is sure of his or her anointing must be able to describe in a few words what his or her own anointing actually is!

Anointing must have Biblical roots

When Jesus described His anointing on that Sabbath day, He read about it from the scriptures, namely Isaiah 61. Therefore, an anointing must always have its roots in the word of God. You can never say that God anointed you to be a bookkeeper in a famous company so that you can earn more money to buy expensive villas and cars while at the same time ignoring the needs of the Kingdom!

Anointing is not a feeling, but a fact!

Jesus did not say: "I feel the Spirit of God is on me and I feel He has anointed me!" When you are anointed, you know it and you have no doubt. You don't even consider for one minute that you are not anointed! The anointing in your life eliminates every doubt and it produces certainty in what you do! The anointing comes on someone when there is the presence of the Holy Spirit. We can feel and sense His presence. We can even see His manifestations.

The presence of the Holy Spirit is the beginning of the anointing because an anointing without the Holy Spirit is fake! The strong presence of the Holy Spirit is the door to God's anointing! Whenever the Holy Spirit is present, you can expect that somebody is being anointed for something sacred and divine!

Anointing has a beginning!

Every person, who is anointed for a certain task by God must know that there is a beginning for the anointing. When was the time you knew in your heart that God anointed you for a certain task in His Kingdom? Can you remember the day? The day when Jesus was officially anointed is registered in the Bible. When He was baptized by John in water, the Spirit of God came upon Him like a dove. The Father said: "This is my beloved son in whom I am pleased" (Matthew 3:13–17). That was the day when the Father anointed Jesus Christ to be the Messiah, the Redeemer of mankind! Of course, from the beginning of time, God the Father had planned for Jesus to be the Redeemer of mankind. But it was on the day of Jesus' anointing that the official work and task of Jesus Christ on earth began!

The day of the anointing means *the day that God started to fulfill His plan through you on earth!* Therefore, you have to know that the anointing comes on you when the proper time has arrived! **You cannot force the anointing of God!**

Anointing lasts for life!

When God anoints you for a certain task, that anointing will last until your task is fulfilled! Therefore, the anointing is functioning 24 hours a day. The anointing has nothing to do with our feelings or the conditions or situations we are dealing with. Many people believe they have to be in a conference or go through special treatments to be anointed! These are false assumptions and ideas. When Jesus healed the sick He was not in a conference. When He raised the dead He did not need any sound system or microphone to boost His anointing! He was anointed 24 hours a day and 7 days a week. The anointing was continually upon Him. As long as we remain in contact with the Holy Spirit and do not sin against Him, the Holy Spirit will never be taken away from us until we have fulfilled the task for which we have been anointed!

The LORD said in Isaiah:

"As the rain and snow come down from heaven, and do not return to it without watering the earth and making it bud and flourish, so that it yields

seed for the sower and bread for the eater, so is my word that goes out from my mouth; it will not return to me empty, but it will accomplish what I desire and achieve the purpose for which I sent it" (Isaiah 55:10–11).

In this passage God is referring to His Word, which is Jesus Christ (John 1). In other words, the LORD is saying that Jesus Christ will not return to Him until He accomplishes His task and purpose on earth. This task and purpose was to destroy sin and Satan, heal the sick and set them free, bring salvation to all mankind, and then die and rise again from the dead and sit at the right hand of God! The same thing is true for us. As long as we are anointed to fulfill His will on earth, we shall not return to Him with empty hands!

4

How to Get the Anointing

The focus of this chapter will be: "*Who gets the anointing? How does it come upon someone and when does it come? What are the patterns for getting the anointing?*" We will be studying the cases of those who were anointed by God in the Old and the New Testaments so that we can understand how the anointing works.

Who Gets the Anointing?

I believe every born again Christian is a candidate for being anointed by God so that he or she can fulfill a life-long mission here on earth. Furthermore, I am convinced that the anointing will not come on a person effortlessly! There is a price tag on the anointing and it is that of a life long commitment, sacrifice and obedience to the will of God through the fellowship and guidance of the Holy Spirit!

There are many candidates for being anointed by God for divine purposes, but there are only a few who are chosen to carry the anointing! We have to pay the price with our lives! Therefore, we do not choose what our anointing will be. It is not up to us. It is God who does it. The only thing we have to do is agree with God and obey Him! Many people live in frustration because they think they are anointed for something when they really aren't. It frustrates them; it hurts them; and it breaks them!

When there is an anointing in your life (or ministry), the heaviest troubles and challenges will not be able to shake you because the anointing covers you and enables you to pass through the "red sea" without being harmed! If you are not anointed for a specific job or task, you may try to pass the "red sea," but just like Pharaoh's army, you will drown and spiritually die there.

The anointing is the legalization and authorization for the task God has called you to do. Lacking this will bring you bitterness and disappointment! The anointing works like the plastic tube that covers electric cables. Touching these cables without the plastic tubes is very dangerous since they may electrocute and kill anyone who touches them! The plastic tube covers the power that goes through it and thus save the lives of those who touch the cable!

How Does the Anointing Come?

Before we were born, God already anointed us in His mind and planned His will concerning us! However, it is our choice whether to let it happen or not! Isaiah wrote: *"Listen to me, you islands, hear this, you distant nations: Before I was born the LORD called me; from my birth he has made mention of my name"* (Isaiah 49:1–2). There is a specific time for the anointing! By this I mean: The day or the specific time you could feel the presence of the Holy Spirit poured in your heart by the Father's will. This can happen in a meeting or on the street or in various extraordinary situations. It is that day when you were convinced deeply in your heart through the Holy Spirit that you had to do the task God was asking you to do! Moreover, the way the anointing comes on us can be different, but there are also similarities. How does it come and how does it happen?

When the priests and the kings were ordained in the Old Testament, they were literally anointed with oil! This anointing with oil consecrated them for their tasks. The anointing with oil, as mystically as it may seem, gave them certain mandates to function and to be different from others!

First of all the anointing comes on God's timing! We can never force the anointing from God! Let us examine the anointing of David in 1 Samuel 16.

"The LORD said to Samuel, *"How long will you mourn for Saul, since I have rejected him as king of*

Israel? Fill your horn with oil and be on your way"
(1 Samuel 16:1). The Lord told Samuel to fill his horn
with oil because He was about to anoint David as
King! Later in the chapter we read that Samuel went
to Bethlehem, to the sons of Jesse: *"When they
arrived, Samuel saw Eliab and thought, 'Surely the
Lord's anointed stands here before the LORD'. But the
LORD said to Samuel, 'Do not consider his appearance or his height, for I have rejected him. The LORD
does not look at the things man looks at. Man looks
at the outward appearance but God looks at the
heart'"* (1 Samuel 16:6–7).

When Samuel saw the older brother of David,
Samuel thought he was the anointed one! But God
didn't choose Eliab. Even though Samuel would have
loved to anoint him, it was deemed possible since
God had someone else in mind — David! God
chooses who is to be anointed! Many times we force
the anointing on our loved ones! We force them to be
someone whom God did not anoint. A lot of pastors'
wives suffer because their husbands want them to
preach and teach simply because they are their
wives! Just because you are the wife of the pastor
does not mean you are anointed to preach!

God commanded Samuel not to look at Eliab's
appearance only! Man looks at the appearance but
the LORD looks at the heart! This is a very important
fact to know about the anointing! God looked at
Eliab's heart and saw that he was not ready. He was

not the one, even though he had the qualifications to be anointed according to Samuel! God does not anoint us because of the qualifications we have or because of the diplomas we have earned, or because we know a lot! No. These things matter but they do not take first place! What matters most is the heart of the anointed one!

It is the heart of man that qualifies him to receive the anointing; it's the heart and the character that flows out of that heart! It is not the education, knowledge, or the skill that matters most!

Before God anoints you for certain things, He will test your heart. He will first check to see whether your heart is good ground to receive His anointing. He will see whether you have the heart of obedience, discipline, and courage! He wants to see the condition of your spirit first! After Samuel saw David, the Lord said, *"'Rise and anoint him; he is the one!' So Samuel took the horn of oil and anointed him in the presence of his brothers, and from that day on the Spirit of the LORD came upon David in power"* (1 Samuel 16: 12–13).

Third, the anointing has to be visible to others. David was anointed in the presence of his brothers! There must be a witness and agreement to someone's anointing! David's anointing was recognized and accepted by Samuel. His brothers witnessed his anointing although they might have envied him! Anointing is not a "one man show business." People must see and recognize the anointing! Even Jesus was anointed in the presence of John the Baptist and the people. Paul was anointed after Ananias prayed for him:

> "But the Lord said to Ananias, 'Go! This man (Paul) is my chosen instrument [in other words my anointed one] to carry my name before the gentiles and their kings and before the people of Israel. I will show him how much he must suffer for my name.' Then Ananias went to the house and entered it. Placing his hands on Saul, he said, 'Brother Saul, the Lord-Jesus, who appeared to you on the road as you were coming here — has sent me so that you may see again and be filled with the Holy Spirit.' Immediately something like scales fell from Saul's eyes, and he could see again. He got up and was baptized, and after taking some food, he regained his strength" (Acts 9:15–19). Once again we see that when God anoints someone for a specific ministry, He will confirm it with someone else present!

Lastly, whenever we read cases of anointing in the Bible, most of the time they come with the Holy Spirit and power! Eventually, it is the Holy Spirit who anoints us and sets us apart for God's divine purpose and plan. Being anointed without both the Holy Spirit and His manifestation is a false anointing! In other words, the one who is anointed has to experience being filled with the Holy Spirit and he should have a constant fellowship and communication with Him. The one who claims to be anointed has to manifest and produce the fruit of the Holy Spirit in his or her life! The anointing on a person's life must be recognized and acknowledged by others, and especially by other men and women of God.

5

WHAT ARE THE RESULTS OF THE ANOINTING?

This chapter is of great significance for everyone who wants to move in the anointing and fulfill his or her God-given calling. Jesus said: "A tree is known by its fruits," and so is the anointing. It is recognized by its results.

What are the results of the anointing on someone's life? What can we expect from our own anointing?

One of the great mistakes people make is that they consider the anointing to be for spiritual activities such as preaching, teaching, and singing only. They limit the anointing only to the four corners of the church and think that when someone preaches well or shouts aloud that that must be the anointing. Others minimize the anointing by believing that whenever someone or something makes them feel good, that is the anointing. Many others are confused and ignorant about the difference between worldly measured success and God's real anointing. For instance, having a mega-church does not necessarily mean that the pastor in that church has a great anointing in his life. Anointing is not measured by outward success. The most important sign of a true anointing is when the anointed one brings to pass what the LORD anointed him for! Whether or not he is anointed for something glorious in the eyes of carnal men is of no consequence. Look at Jesus for example, He was indeed anointed and yet He had to die in a cruel manner on the cross. The Bible says they gathered around Him and ridiculed Him saying, "If He is the Son of God, why can He not rescue himself." Many doubted Him because they wanted to see a glorious Jesus who would call upon the armies of angels, strike the enemy, and rescue Jerusalem and all who believed. To them this was what a great anointing should be used for. People wanted a great spectacle or a huge Hollywood event, but this was not what Jesus was anointed for. Nowadays, many people are looking for big entertainment in the Body of Christ, but they forget that the anointing is not a show! The question is, "How can we distinguish between a false and a true anointing?"

Below are some of the important points that indicate a true anointing upon your life:

- *The Anointing transforms your life*
- *The Anointing always has an exact job (action) description*

- *The Anointing brings forth the miraculous*
- *The Anointing breaks the yoke so that you can serve God freely*
- *The Anointing attracts people*

The Anointing Transforms Your Life

A transformed life is the greatest sign of a true anointing. Once God affirms His anointing and sets you apart for His purpose, your life will be turned upside down. You will experience a radical change and transformation on many levels including your character and attitude. Jesus was a carpenter before He was officially anointed by God. But when His time came, He was changed. He was not the same carpenter anymore. His words were stated with power and authority. Something happened in the heavenly realms when Christ was anointed by God. The heavens moved and opened and the LORD announced publicly: "This is My Son in whom I delight." Then the Holy Spirit came like a dove upon Jesus. He was anointed! He was not the carpenter anymore. Can you imagine what kind of authority an ordinary carpenter might have in a society like ancient Israel, maybe none. A carpenter is carpenter and not a teacher, a politician, or a rabbi. How could Jesus the carpenter have so much authority that the educated rabbis and Roman officers feared Him so much? What gave Him such power that by His words the sick and the lepers were healed, the blind could see, and the dead could rise? What changed? What was different about Him? How did He go from being a carpenter to being the Savior of mankind? **It was the anointing!** When you are anointed, you are changed. The way you talk and the way you move and live are different. Life is flowing in you. You are not the same! However, be aware that there is always a preparation period between being anointed and actually moving in that anointing. You can be anointed but still not be moving in the anointing.

Moving in the anointing means you are practicing what God has anointed you to do. This is what David did. Samuel anointed David as king, but it took a while before David really moved in the anointing and practiced his kingship. There was a desert period in between. I believe there is a period between being anointed and moving in (practicing) the anointing. I call this period "the desert period." It is in the desert that God teaches us so many things such as perseverance, patience, love, forgiveness, etc. He is also building a new transformed character within us. This desert period is different for everyone, but it is still important for all of us. Therefore, the anointing must change our character both spiritually and naturally.

If you think you are working under the anointing of God but you still have a lifestyle that is different from what Christ wants, then either you are not anointed or you are polluting the anointing God has given you. When you mix your anointing with unbiblical habits and unpleasant character, the anointing will be gradually taken away from you.

The Anointing always Has an Exact Job (Action) Description

The anointed ones do not doubt; they have a specific job and calling from God in their lives. They are chosen for it and they are even ready to die for it. If you are anointed to do something for God, then you know for sure in your heart what you are supposed to be doing.

I have encountered so many people who ask for God's anointing. They are anointing-addicted people. They spend most of their time lying on the floors of meeting halls, and yet there's no movement or action that indicates they are serving God in any capacity. All they do is get high in the presence of God. But when you ask them, "For what purpose are you anointed? They have nothing to say! If you move from person to person or from meeting to meeting to get the anointing, then something is very wrong. Anointing without action is dead.

You don't get anointed for the sake of anointing; anointing requires action. Now, I don't mean that you have to jump into work the minute you receive God's anointing. As I mentioned earlier, there has to be a preparation and desert period involved!

The Anointing Brings Forth the Miraculous

When someone is anointed by God, then the miraculous starts working in that person's life. By miraculous, I don't only mean the opening of blind eyes or raising the dead. Of course, these are parts of the miraculous, but the Holy Spirit is not limited to things such as healings or casting out devils.

By miraculous, I am referring to the things that are not possible. With the anointing, the impossible becomes possible. The anointing enables you to do great and impossible things. Let us take a look at David and Goliath. When did David kill Goliath? Was it before Samuel anointed David or after? Of course it was after! David was anointed first with oil on his head and body. The anointing gave David the right from heaven to kill Goliath. God chose him to succeed Saul as king. Saul had all the armies behind him. He had the best weapons and defense, but he still could not defeat Goliath because he had already lost his anointing. He didn't have the anointing or the right anymore. On the other hand, David, without any advanced weapon or proper clothing, confronted Goliath. And with just a few stones from the river, he was able to defeat and kill Goliath.

Like David's victory over Goliath, the anointing enables you to have victory over every situation. The anointing makes you do extraordinary things. I know somebody who planned to learn a musical instrument.

She had no experience and she had never played any instrument before. But then she attended classes and tried to learn. Once in a prayer meeting, I sensed that the Lord wanted me to anoint her and set her apart for playing that instrument so she could glorify the Lord and usher in the presence of God in meetings. So, I anointed her as the Lord instructed me and the anointing came upon her officially. She only had attended 10 lessons, but suddenly something changed in her when she began to play. She dared and she could do it. Some professional musicians told me that for a beginner, she was doing great. Of course, she did not become a professional musician immediately, but the process was now in motion!

The Anointing Attracts People

Those who are anointed have a special God-given charisma. This is not natural charisma but God-given Charisma. These men and women attract others to them; people become interested in them and they feel something fresh in them. When these anointed men or women speak or act under the anointing, people listen or watch more carefully. Suddenly, the atmosphere changes when they enter the room. Pay attention! Jesus had no natural charisma at all. Even the Bible says He had nothing in Him to attract others. But Jesus was under the anointing; He had a God-given charisma that attracted people to Him.

Furthermore, by being under the anointing I do not mean you have to be strange in order to attract people. On the contrary, you have to be yourself. Many people are confused in this matter. They think that when they change their voice or the manner of their walking this must mean that their charisma is under the anointing. This is wrong! Charisma under the anointing is not bound to any dress or any fashion code in the world. Either you have it or you don't!

The Anointing Breaks the Yoke

The anointed ones are free people. There is a common statement in the body of Christ: The anointing breaks the yoke. We have to realize that we cannot serve God in slavery; we must first be free. We must be free from the things that kept us in bondage. Anointed people have to be free from bitterness, anger, sexual immorality, slanderous talk, and lack of honest love toward others.

Anointing comes from the Holy Spirit; therefore, the anointed ones have to manifest the fruits of the Holy Spirit in their lives. Being anointed for whatever purpose has to produce the fruits of the Holy Spirit.

"The acts of the sinful nature are obvious: sexual immorality, impurity, and debauchery; idolatry and witchcraft; hatred, discord, jealousy, fits of rage, selfish ambition, dissensions, factions and envy; drunkenness, orgies, and the like. I warn you, as I did before, that those who live like this will not inherit

the Kingdom of God. But the fruit of the Spirit is love, joy, peace, patience, kindness, goodness, faithfulness, gentleness and self-control. Against such things there is no law!" (Galatians 5:19–23).

If someone is bound to the sinful nature and he claims to be anointed, either he is wrong and falsely anointed, or he is anointed but will gradually lose it if he does not change. Living with a yoke means living in these sinful acts or lifestyle. Samson was an anointed man of God, but he was yoked with sin. Gradually, he lost his anointing to the point where he was imprisoned. The moment he repented and asked God to restore him, he was able to get his strength back and knock down the pillars of the tower. The entire building crashed and all his enemies died.

Lastly, The devil can only imitate the miraculous. He is not able to imitate the true fruits of the Holy Spirit. He can never imitate the love of God, His kindness, His patience, and all that the Spirit has given to the anointed ones. Honestly, I do not care how much people consider themselves to be anointed. The first thing I look at is whether I can find some fruits of the Holy Spirit in their lives. If not, I have to doubt the condition of their anointing. Anointing enables us to do the works of God; it is the authorized license to our calling. In the next chapters, I will be guiding you step-by-step so you can discover your calling and learn how to use the tools you need to be effective.

PART III

DISCOVERING & RESHAPING YOUR CALL

6

WHAT IS A CALLING?

Once a person is saved, he or she must grow to fulfill God's purposes. There are so many disillusioned Christians who after being saved stay so relaxed thinking that Jesus will soon return and bring them into an eternal holiday in heaven. They claim they are saved anyway. *If these ideas were true, why did God not bring us to heaven immediately when we became Christians?* The answer is simple. From the time we were born again, God already designed His plans for our lives. His plans are our callings!

What is a calling then?

A calling is a divine task that God has placed in your heart in order to fulfill His plans on earth through you in your generation.

Based upon this definition, I would like to discuss what the crucial term "calling" means. Understanding what a "calling" is is very important for knowing the validity of our calling in our lives.

Calling Is Divine

First, a calling is a divine task or a holy assignment. By divine task, I mean a task that is inspired and fueled by God! A calling is the task God has placed in your heart. Along with it, He also gave you the passion, the anointing, and the tools to fulfill it! For example, if someone says: "My calling in life is to earn millions and establish my company worldwide so that I may gain esteem, respect, and honor from people. I also want to secure a royal life for my children." This might be a calling for this person, but it is not a divine calling. It is a calling based solely on personal desires and interests.

Sometimes a calling may seem divine because it appears to have a sense of religiosity, but it still may not be divine because it is not inspired by the Holy Spirit. Instead, it is a person's own desire and thinking. For example, there are people whom God never called to be pulpit ministers, but they are in the pulpit because of their own ideas and desires. Most of the time their ministries end up in disappointment and frustration. A calling cannot be forced on anybody, either by God or any person! A calling is divine and it requires the free will of every man.

Calling Bears Good Fruit

The sign of a true calling is in its fruit. We might have the passion for a certain calling, but if God does not bless it, it will give no fruit at all nor will it bear good fruits. God is the starter and finisher of all things. When He starts something with your agreement, He will make sure that you will be able to finish it and produce fruits that last! Jesus tells us that every good tree is known by its fruit; a good tree will give good fruit, and so it is with choosing the right calling. It will produce good fruit. I have met many people who have been strongly disappointed simply because they failed to listen to their true calling. In chapter seven, I will be discussing in detail how we may find our errors and be able to choose the right calling for our lives!

Calling Is God's Plan through You

We have to understand that a calling is about fulfilling God's plans on earth through His people. When Jesus taught His disciples to pray, He asked to them to pray like this: *"Our father who is in heaven hallowed be your name, your kingdom come, your will be done, here on earth as it is in heaven"* (Matthew 6:9–10). God wants to establish His Kingdom here on earth through us. God has certain plans and certain strategies for the world in every generation, and He needs His people to be willing to be used.

If every born again Christian does the Father's will, we will rapidly be able to reach the world with the Gospel of Jesus Christ. The Father's will is our calling! Remember that you are needed NOW! TODAY! You don't have to be a pulpit minister to have a calling in your life. God can use you in many ways, either in the world, the marketplace, or from behind the pulpit.

Calling Must Lead to the Great Commission

Many people make a great mistake in thinking that evangelism is equal to the Great Commission. This is wrong! Let us examine the relationship between our Calling and the Great Commission given by Jesus two thousand years ago:

> *"All authority in heaven and on earth has been given to me. Therefore, go and make disciples of all nations, baptizing them in the name of the Father and the Son and the Holy Spirit, teach them what I have commanded you. Surely I will be with you always, to the very end of the age"* (Matthew 28:18–20).

The Great Commission consists of four important components: "Go," "Make Disciples of Nations," "Baptize," and "Teach!" Every calling must either lead directly or indirectly to fulfilling the Great Commission or at least completing one of the four components of the Great Commission. Otherwise, there is something wrong with that calling.

For example, when someone says his calling is to help the poor, the question is this: Does this calling end up directly or indirectly in fulfilling the Great Commission? Does helping the poor witness directly or indirectly the Gospel of Jesus Christ? Does it make disciples? Does it prepare the way for others to hear the message of hope and love? If not, what then is the difference between this and UNICEF or the United Nations?

Another example: when someone says his calling is singing for the Lord, that person should ask himself whether or not his singing results in fulfilling one or two of the components of the Great Commission. Singing can lead people to Christ, teach people, and bring them into the presence of God. It can even baptize people in the Spirit. If someone sings but says, "Well, I love to sing for myself and bring myself in the presence of God and feel good," that person does not have a calling!

Calling Fits in God's Government

In chapter one, I mentioned a very important fact: the Church represents the body of Christ, or the Kingdom of God here on earth. I also mentioned the five-fold ministry, as written in Ephesians 4:11–13. I added a sixth ministry and I termed it as the Ministry of God's

People. God's five-fold ministry is there to equip, teach, and mobilize God's people to fulfill their callings.

Therefore, every calling needs to move through the channels of God-given authority and government. Jesus said: "I am the vine; you are the branches. If a man remains in me and I in him, he will bear much fruit. Apart from me you can do nothing. If anyone does not remain in me, he is like a branch that is thrown away and withers; such branches are picked up, thrown into the fire and burned" (John 15:5–6). Many Christians fail in this area. They think they have a calling, but they do not want to be mentored, advised, or belong to a spiritual family. They never want to connect and network with others. They like to work in isolation because they don't need anybody's help. They don't even want to be under someone's leadership.

If you want to fulfill your calling, you have to connect to the five-fold ministry and make sure you are trained and equipped to fulfill your calling. By connecting, I don't mean that these ministries should dominate you or dictate you, what you have to do or not! By being connected I mean: to network with, to recognize the five-fold ministry and to cooperate with, as far as you can, not by force or by manipulation. You need to be connected with pastors and make sure they pastor you biblically. In the same way, you need apostles and prophets in order to receive guidance and advice in times of need. Be open to the teachers so you do not fall away from the truth. They teach you to be strong in your foundations! Connect also to evangelists so that they may remind you about the Gospel and your duty towards the Great Commission.

Some people choose to be lonely runners. They do not want to cooperate with other people. There are also people who would rather work with leaders in high positions than with those in low positions, within a team. These types of people will end up in disappointment and their calling will fail one day!

Calling Fits in God's Generational Plan

In every generation, God has His agenda and He wants His people to be involved in His plans. Just like every person has a destiny, every generation and every nation has a destiny as well. Time after time, the Bible speaks about the destiny of nations. You have to realize that you are living in a specific time in history with certain ethnic, racial, and cultural standards. This is the will of God for you. Even the color of your skin is designed by God for a purpose. You are specially designed by God so that He may use you for your generation. Realizing this will help you love yourself and love who you are culturally, ethnically, and geographically! The question now is this: does our calling fit into God's generational plan? Remember that what was considered a calling eight hundred years ago might be totally useless today! For example, it is unreasonable to think that your calling is to become a monk so you can write English bibles with your bare hands and distribute them because there is a shortage of bibles today! This way of producing bibles was effective a thousand years ago, but it is a waste of time today because of technology.

Let me give you another example. I believe that Martin Luther King served the Lord in his generation. His time was one of the darkest periods in the history of United States of America. African Americans were discriminated against in every aspect. They were brutally treated, murdered, and assassinated. It was something like the apartheid that occurred in South Africa.

Amidst of all these social injustices and maltreatment, God the Father raised up a man, a reverend, from among the black people. His name was Martin Luther King. When God formed this man in his mother's womb, He knew for what reason He created him. He made him to stand up for the rights of black people in America and to set them free. Imagine if Martin would not have listened to the voice of Jesus and did not become a born again Christian. God would not have used him since God does not force His plans upon anybody! Dr. King's calling fit perfectly in the generational plan and strategy of God. His calling was wired to the Great Commission because he taught us what Jesus had taught the disciples. Dr. King's calling did not deny the authenticity of the Church as being God's government here on earth!

Truly, every Christian fits into God's generational plan whether they are conscious about it or not! The choice is ours to fit into it or to deny it!

Calling Should Be in Agreement

In various times, the Bible speaks about the power of agreement. Jesus Himself said: "When two or three come together and agree in My Name, and pray, the Father in heaven will give them anything they ask for! The book of Amos says: *"How can two men walk together unless they are agreed?* (Amos 3:3). Remember, no one can force a calling on you! Maybe a pastor or a leader thinks he knows what your calling is. But the first thing you must do is check whether you have the passion and burning desire for that or not. If not, then the calling is not for you. If it is for you, then even if you have no passion for it, the Holy Spirit will touch you in a way that automatically lets you feel the urge and call in your life. As the body of Christ we need to wake up; we need to be in the places where God has appointed us to be. We need a spiritual exodus; we must return to our callings and fulfill them in the Name of the Lord!

There are people whom God has never called to be a pulpit pastor; however, they have self-appoint themselves. There are some who are called to function in the marketplace yet because of some preacher who told them to leave their workplaces and get into the fulltime ministry, they lost their jobs, talents, connections, and skills. They left everything to become a fulltime pulpit minister when God did not ask them to do that. Now they are frustrated and have not achieved anything yet! Let us get ready; let us shake the devil's kingdom by simply being in the position God has planned for us!

Checklist

Check whether your calling is in agreement with the following criteria:

•	My calling is divine	☐ yes	☐ no
•	My calling bears good fruit	☐ yes	☐ no
•	My calling is God's plan through me	☐ yes	☐ no
•	My calling leads to the Great Commission	☐ yes	☐ no
•	My calling fits in God's Kingdom Network	☐ yes	☐ no
•	My calling is designed for my generation	☐ yes	☐ no
•	My calling is in agreement with God	☐ yes	☐ no

If all your answers are yes, then you are on the right track. Continue fulfilling your call. If not, then you have to pray and find out where you are lacking or why you are coming up short! In the next chapter, I will be giving you some practical tools that will enable you to identify your calling so you can be even more effective than before.

7

DISCOVERING YOUR CALLING

This chapter will focus on discovering or reshaping your calling. Keeping the information of the previous chapters in our minds and spirits, we are now ready to take off. I believe you already have an idea of what your calling is. However, you might have some questions about the validity of your calling. Have you ever asked yourself, "Am I doing the right thing or am I doing what He has called me to do?" This chapter will help you to discover your calling and eliminate any doubts you might have. This chapter will train you to become specialized in your calling.

What You Have in the Natural

You may have heard this verse: "first the natural then the spiritual." This is of great value for us to begin with. Understanding this truth will make you see things beyond the borders of their scope and limitations.

This will make you move into a new dimension of understanding both in the natural and in the spiritual world.

From the time of our biological births, God has given us certain talents and abilities. Our parents, relatives, friends, teachers, and our socio-cultural environment either helped us develop or waste these God-given talents and gifts. That is why the childhood period is very crucial to a person's life. It is in this period that the qualities of the child will be established and grow until he or she becomes a responsible individual in society. We must realize that it is the will of God for every individual to become born again and every person in his or her lifetime will have various opportunities to receive Christ as their Lord and Savior. Keeping this fact in mind, we then have to realize that by being born again we are entering God's Kingdom. And as we enter, we bring with us our own package of talents, abilities, and experiences, whether they are good or bad. These things we bring with us are compared to raw materials that God uses one by one; He will reshape and reform them and prepare you for the calling He has for you! Therefore, our life experiences and background are very crucial for our place in the kingdom.

Before you knew the Lord, what were your talents? What did you have to offer? Were they good or bad? These are very important questions in analyzing and discovering your calling. Go over the following questions and write your answers down on a piece of paper:

- When you were a child between the ages of 0–5, what were you good at?
- If you do not remember, go and ask someone older who remembers.
- What talents did you have between the ages of 6–10? What did you want to be back then? What subjects interested you the most?
- What were your talents, gifts, and life experiences between the ages of 11–18? What dreams did you have for the future? What were your ambitions, characteristics, hobbies, and the things you were passionate for?
- What kind of education, work experience, and talents did you have until the day you became born again?
- This is the most important question: what were you busy with (kind of job, talents, etc.) during the first years of your new life in the Kingdom?

Many people quote the Bible verse that says: "When you are in the Lord you are a new creation, the old has gone the new has come (2 Corinthians 5:17). Of course, this is true and yet many misinterpret this verse. Some people think that by becoming a Christian, God immediately deletes all their information from their brains and installs the latest operation system software so that they can forget their own identity and live happily ever after! The reality is different! We become born again Christians and we are happy for a couple of months or even years, but after that the real life begins.

Fortunately, some have a relatively good background such as a solid family support system and education while others are entering the Kingdom with a huge package of disappointments, tragic happenings, and horrible experiences. Being born again does not wipe away the memories of the past; it will help you live with them in victory all the time.

As I mentioned earlier, what you had in the natural before you were born into the spiritual is very important for your calling. Moses is a perfect example! Moses was taken from the river and grew up as a prince in Egypt! When he was still young, he had this passion for the Jewish people who were then slaves in Egypt. Even though he grew up as an Egyptian prince, in his heart he was aware that he was a Jew. This passion caused him to get into many troubles, one of which was murdering an Egyptian in defense of a fellow Jew:

> *"One day, after Moses had grown up, he went out where his own people were and watched them at their labor. He saw an Egyptian beating a Hebrew, one of his own people. Glancing this way and that and seeing no one, he killed the Egyptian and hid him in the sand. The next day he went out and saw two Hebrews fighting. 'Why are you fighting your*

*fellow Hebrew?' The man said: '**who made you
ruler and judge over us?** Are you thinking of
killing me as you killed the Egyptian?' Then Moses
was afraid and thought 'what I did must have
become known'"* (Exodus 2:11–15, emphasis
added).

Moses' passion for Israel and for righteousness
made him a murderer! Moses fought for his people.
Notice what the Hebrew said to Moses: *"Who made
you ruler and judge over us?"* Those days Moses was
not even called by God officially and yet his passion
and love was there within him. This Hebrew even
spoke something prophetic at him. True enough, Moses
became the redeemer, the ruler, and the judge of the
Hebrews and led his people out of Egyptian slavery. Do
you remember the moment when Moses was called
into the ministry? In Exodus 3, we read about his burning bush experience. For the first time in his life, he
encountered God and accepted him as his Lord. In our
New Testament terminology, we can say that he gave his
life to God. This event can be compared with us being
born again and accepting Christ as our Lord and Savior.

Immediately after recognizing and accepting God
in his life, the Lord gave Moses his assignment: "Go
and set My people free!" Moses asked the Lord how
he could do this. Then in chapter 4, the Lord asked
Moses the most historic and well-known question:
"'What is in your hand?' 'A staff,' Moses replied.

'Then throw it on the ground' the Lord said." Moses threw the staff on the ground and it turned into a snake, then Moses grabbed the snake's tail and it turned into a staff again.

What was in Moses' hand when he met God? A staff! The staff was the tool he used to lead the flock of sheep and goats in the mountains. Now after his encounter with God, this very same staff became the symbol and the sign of God's anointing and calling in his life by which he would lead the flock of God, Israel. Moses remained a shepherd, but he would no longer herd sheep and goats. He would now shepherd the beloved nation of the Lord, and in all these, the staff would become a source of power and God's sign to Moses. You see, there's a link between Moses' passion and love for the Jews that goes back to his youth when he was being groomed as a prince. Now, he still remains as a fighter and redeemer for Israel although at a totally different level. He now received the confirmation of his calling!

Let us go back to you now. When you gave your life to Christ, the moment you had your personal burning bush experience, what did you have in your hands? What was your staff and what were the dreams of your youth? What did you have in your hands the moment you were born again? I am sure that the thing you had in your 'hand' will become a key to your calling! 'The staff' could be many things and it may differ from person to person. What was your 'staff' back then? I still remember my 'staff.' When I was seven years old, I was already a leader in my school. I rallied the students for riots. When I was twelve years old I founded my own political group at school and was arrested. Between the ages of fourteen and seventeen, I was involved in youth leadership for a very famous political party in exile. I met the last Prime Minister of my country when it was still a monarchy. At the age of twenty, I started loving Africa deeply. My dream was to study and go to Africa and serve that continent. I loved black and reggae music. That is why my friends called me 'the Rasta Man.' Later, I started to become interested in Asian culture and I married a Korean. I studied culture and global sociology to understand people.

Between the ages of twelve and eighteen, many people asked me to speak in public and at some political gatherings. I was so good for my age that some people stood on their feet and applauded. This ability was my 'staff,' the thing I had in my hands when I gave my life to Christ. Today, I am still doing the things I used to do, but on a different level. After I gave my life to Christ, God opened my bag and took my staff. He turned it upside down in order to use it in a different way. Remember, you can never change your past, but you can turn it upside down. The staff of Moses was the same, but the Lord transformed it. Let the Lord transform your dreams, your visions, and your past, including the positive and even the negative things in your life. Therefore, I ask you this question again: What did you have in your hands, the moment you were born again?

There is a problem of ignorance about the 'staff' we bring with us during our spiritual birth! There is a group of Christians, who throw away their past, their talents, and their God-given abilities. They'd rather pick up somebody else's 'staff' and try to use it as if it were their own. No wonder things do not work out for them! They never succeed! They try to imitate somebody else's anointing and calling. Therefore, they fail and become frustrated. You have to realize that you are unique and your calling is unique. God did not ask some people to be pastors. Yet, they want to become pastors so badly that they even imitate famous men of God. After a while, they see that it does not work so they quit. But by then it is already too late to reverse their lives!

The Kingdom of God needs all types of people who are called for all types of callings. Some may be involved in the five-fold ministry and some may be in the ministry of God's people. Some are movie makers, some are politicians, some are cooks, some are taxi drivers, and others do a hundred other things.

There is another group who throw their 'staffs' on the ground, but they never pick them up. Instead, they allow fear to consume them believing that God might not use them, and so they fail. It is better, though, to try and fail than to do nothing at all!

Lastly, there are those who throw their 'staffs' on the ground and dare to pick them up from the tail and use them for God's glory. Take your 'staff' by its tail! Do not fear! Do not let your dreams be taken away from you! You are the same person, the same body, the same past, and yet you are different because you have encountered the power of the Holy Spirit. Use the things of your past to advance the Kingdom. Go forth!

Once I met a young girl who was saved through my ministry. After a while, I noticed certain disorders in her character. She would not associate with fellow brothers in the church. She would not even mention the word "father," because she had been physically molested and abused by her own father for at least two or three years. Since then, she hated men. After many prayers and much counseling, she began to heal. I helped her to not run away from her past even though her past was a nightmare. As strange and tragic it may sound, I taught her that her experience was her 'staff.' She has to live with it for the rest of her life because the memory is there, but this time she takes this 'staff' from the tail and masters it because the Lord has called her to save many others who are in the tyranny of child molestation and abuse. It takes pain to understand pain! I sincerely advised her that now she can ruin the kingdom of Satan from the front-line because she knows the ways of Satan in that specific area! Today, this girl is a missionary and a minister. She's helping, supporting and nursing people who have the same problem. You can never free others if you are not free yourself!

David is another interesting example from the Bible. When Samuel anointed David with oil and revealed to him that he would be the next King of Israel (God's calling), he (David) was busy tending the flock. What was his 'staff'? It was his 'leading the flock.' David was a shepherd and he was also a warrior. He had already killed a lion and a bear while he was tending the flock. He also killed Goliath. David was a fighter by nature. Therefore, God used him later to be the King of Israel to bring victory to the nation while shepherding the people (1 Samuel 16, 17; and 2 Samuel 2, 5).

Peter is another good example. Peter was a fisherman when Jesus called him to be one of His disciples. Jesus said to him: "From now on you will catch men" (Luke 5:10). It was then that Jesus Christ called Peter into evangelism, the ministry of "fishing for men." What did Peter have when Jesus called him into ministry? What was his 'staff'? It was the fact that he was a fisherman. Normally, fishermen dare to travel to many parts of the sea regardless of the dangers. Did he not travel to many places to preach the gospel?

Let's take a look at our families. It is very important for parents to find out at an early age the abilities and the talents that their own children posses so that they may be able to develop them. One day the Lord will use each ability and skill when He calls them into the Kingdom! In the same way, pastors and leaders need to realize that newly born Christians have their own natural abilities, and therefore, they might be beneficial to the Kingdom if these abilities are tapped properly and trained accordingly. They can be mobilized for the ministry of GOD'S PEOPLE.

Is there a Burning Passion within You?

In these times of apathy and a feeling-less society, the body of Christ needs to be filled with godly passion in order to be able to fulfill the Father's will here on earth. God does not dwell in automatic actions that are based on formulas and laws. God looks at the heart of man. Many times, we tend to do things out of routine or out of obligation. The passion is gone. When you have a calling in your life, you have to have godly passion. This passion will be with you until you die! It was not David the warrior who pleased God the most. Rather, it was David the worshiper, the passionate man, who pleased the heart of God.

God wants you to burn with passion for the things He has called you to do! Many have lost their passion in life. It is time for you to restore that passion. Maybe you need to ask yourself, "Why has my passion died?" "Why has the flame faded out?" There are many reasons for this. Sometimes the worries of life and ministry burden us so much that we have the tendency to feel down and empty. Remember, Peter sank into the sea when he saw the big waves coming! What do you think occurred in Peter's heart and mind that moment he decided to walk on water? Did he not think that he could actually drown into the depths of the sea and die? Or was he stupid enough to think he could defy gravity? What was the power behind Peter's decision to step out of the boat and take the risk? The answer is Peter's passion: "Lord if it is you," Peter replied, "tell me to come (call me) to come to you on the water" (Matthew 14:28). This is passion. This is the burning desire of Peter to be called by Jesus. It is this passion that led him to walk on the water toward Jesus. A passionate response to God's call in your life will bring forth a great impact. Passion enables you to walk on waters and nothing will be able to harm you. We should not look at the waves of life. They are stumbling blocks for fulfilling our destiny; they kill our passion and our love to fulfill our calling.

Second, our passion dies when we forget to be like children through the years of being "in the Lord."

"Let the little children come to me and do not hinder them, for the kingdom of God belongs to such as these. I tell you the truth, anyone who will not receive the kingdom of God like a little child will never enter it" (Mark 10:14–15).

Jesus said: "Let them come." This is the sign of a calling. Receiving the Kingdom of God means having a part, a function, a calling in that Kingdom. A calling without fitting into God's Kingdom is not a calling at all! How can you enter it? You enter it when you become like a little child filled with passion, life, love, and honesty with God! When we just become born again, the childlike passion burns within us. However, experience shows that the more we grow in our knowledge of theology and doctrines, the more they get a hold of us. We forget to be childlike. We forget that God can make miracles. We forget that He is in control of our calling in life; we just need to be as simple as a child. When we refuse to do this, the stress and burdens of life will come on us heavily and we will easily lose the passion.

Never lose your childlike passion because of any doctrine or man-made theology. God values your passion more than all those things! Ask yourself, "Do you still have the burning passion of God's calling in your life?" Do everything with passion and love for Christ!

8

STEPPING INTO YOUR CALLING

Finding out about your calling is one thing, but stepping into your calling is another. Only knowing your calling is not sufficient; you need to do it and put it into correct practice. Every great journey starts with a small step. In the following paragraphs, we will be dealing with important facts that we need to know in order to be able to step into our calling.

Calculate the Costs

Once, Jesus Christ spoke the following words: *"If anyone comes to me and does not hate his father and mother, his wife and children, his brothers and sisters-yes, even his own life-he cannot be my disciple. Anyone who does not carry his cross and follow me cannot be my disciple. Suppose one of you wants to build a tower. Will he not first sit down and estimate the cost to see if he has enough money to complete it? For if he lays the foundation and is still not able to finish it, everyone who sees it will ridicule him, saying, 'This fellow began to build and was not able to finish.' Or suppose a king is about to go to war against another king. Will he not first sit down and consider whether he is able with ten thousand men to oppose the one coming against him with twenty thousand? If he is not able, he will send a delegation while the other is still a long way off and will ask for terms of peace. In the same way, any of you who do not give up everything he has cannot be my disciple"* (Luke 14:25–33).

Many people are confused, because they misunderstand the above Bible passage. They think Jesus is teaching us to hate our families and beloved ones. This is not true! Jesus never taught us these things, but what He emphasizes is this: if we want to follow Him, we need to face the challenge, and we need to estimate the costs of being His disciple. Notice that Jesus said: "Estimate the cost." Have you estimated the cost of being a disciple of Jesus Christ? In other words, you have to realize that your calling is not an emotional thing that you can take lightly. This is a serious matter! This might even cost you your life, your possessions, your habits, and your pleasant daily life activities.

Are you ready to pay the price for your calling? It doesn't matter how big or small your calling may seem to you. Your calling is not a hobby, but it is your life for

Christ! If you are ready to sacrifice everything for your God-given calling, then you are ready. Otherwise, you need to pray more!

Just Start

There is a time for everything. Our spiritual journey has a starting point. These days there are so many Christians who have all the information, all the right desires, and passion. They have even received the anointing for their calling from God, but they still wait and confuse themselves with words like these: "I am still praying for it." Or, "I am still waiting for the Lord's green light." They wait and wait. They go from seminary to seminary, from course to course, but they still do nothing. When you know your calling and what you need to do, do not waste your time. Just do it. Take your first step. Step into obedience and the Holy Spirit will lead you and show you what to do.

- If Abraham did not start the journey, he would not have become the father of many nations.
- If Peter did not step out of the boat, he could not have walked on the water.
- If Moses did not go back to Egypt, he could not have led the Israelites out of slavery in Egypt.
- If the Israelites did not walk on the Jordan River, the river would not have opened.

When you start, try to see your place in the God-given spiritual government and God's Great Commission! Don't start without a solid foundation and without an aim. Build upon the foundation of God's Commission and Government!

Every Great Thing Starts Small

After taking your first step, realize that all great things start small! You can never achieve great things if you are not faithful in the small things. Many people live in confusion because they want to be on top immediately! God, though, cooks us slowly from the inside out and He gradually prepares us for greater things. Remember, God is not in a hurry! He has all the time in the world. He owns the time! You need to realize that 'calling' is a lifetime work with a process of growth. Your calling is like a small baby who undergoes growth and development. However, this growth all depends on how you nourish and train the baby!

For example, if your calling is to preach the word of God in a mighty way, God will bring situations where you need to preach to one or two people. God will test you and see how you will handle these two people. If you handle your assignment with love and passion, then He will entrust you with more people! If you get disappointed because you expected more, then you have a problem. How can you preach to

10,000 people if you are not ready to preach to 2 people?

Your calling is to be in God's People Ministry by being involved in the administration of your church. How can you do this if you are not even able to handle your own paperwork at home? Your calling might be handling God's finances for great evangelistic projects. Great evangelistic crusades need large amounts of money too. God will never entrust you with big numbers if you are not faithful with the little money you received!

David is a clear example of this. Prior to killing Goliath, David had killed a lion and a bear. God trained David to destroy armies by thousands and ten thousands because he was ready for it. From being a lion and bear killer, he was promoted to be the Goliath killer. And from being the Goliath killer, he turned to be an army killer and after that he became the king of Israel!

We need to humble ourselves and be faithful with the small assignments we receive from God. Only faithfulness is proof of our promotion in our spiritual life.

Holy Spirit Our Mentor

In John 14:15–31, Jesus gave us the promise of the Holy Spirit. Jesus spoke of the Holy Spirit as the One who is the same as He. The Holy Spirit is the Counselor, the Teacher, and the God who knows all truths. The body of Christ needs the Holy Spirit like never before. The Holy Spirit is the coequal, coexisting personality of the triune God. Jesus ascended to the Father so that the Holy Spirit would come down. When you allow Him, the Holy Spirit will shape you, develop you, and of course, help you.

There are certain facts you need to know about the function of the Holy Spirit. These will help you work out your calling:

- The Holy Spirit never speaks against the written Constitution, the Holy Bible; instead, He will make sure that the scriptures will be fulfilled through your calling.
- The Holy Spirit never asks you to do things that are not fitted in God's Church (God's government), God's Great Commission, and God's word.
- The Holy Spirit never brings disorder in God's anointed Church and government which is within the framework of the five-fold ministry!
- The Holy Spirit leads you to work in harmony with others in the ministry both on a local and universal level.

Spiritual Mentors

Many people make a great mistake by saying: "I only need the Holy Spirit and I do not need anybody to mentor me." In contrast, the apostle Paul said: *"Even though you have ten thousand of guardians in Christ, you do not have many fathers, for in Christ I became your father through the gospel. Therefore I urge you to imitate me"* (1 Corinthians 4:15–16).

In other words, Paul considered himself as their mentor. To the Church in Rome he said: *"I long to see you that I may impart to you some spiritual gift to make you strong — that is, that you and I may mutually encouraged by each other's faith"* (Romans 1:11). Every person who is called must have a spiritual mentor alongside the Holy Spirit. It doesn't matter who you are and how good you are. You need spiritual mentors who will strengthen you, encourage you, and impart their gifts to you. This brings unity and order in the Kingdom.

If you think you know better and you refuse to learn from your spiritual mentors, then there is something wrong with you. Following their examples will help you learn from their faith and life including both their mistakes and successes. Be humble and learn! You must never stop learning! Go behind those who have inspired you and learn well from them.

Have No Fear

If God is with us, who can be against us? When you know your calling and when you know for what purpose you are born, you will have no fear. In God there is no fear. God has called you; He gave you the mandate. He has anointed you to do the impossible. The biggest enemy of Christians is fear. Fear aborts every vision in us. Fear kills every dream and every dreamer. It is better to step into our calling and fail, than to do nothing and still fail! We only live once. We have to fulfill our destiny. Go for your calling!

Picture the End

See the end of your calling. Imagine what would happen if you fully completed your calling in life! What would your environment look like when your calling is fulfilled! How many lives would have been changed and impacted! Many Christians with a calling live only for today! Remember we are those who have to influence the world. We are Christ's people here on earth. Many of us do not pass the walls of blessings. As soon as a little achievement comes or a small measure of success shows up, we stop right there! We are satisfied too soon, and because of this attitude, we are not able see the future and move beyond it.

Abraham was not a father yet when God called him to be the father of many nations. But God showed him his end; He made him look at the stars in the sky. Even though it seemed he was going nowhere, having no child, but yet the Lord spoke to him and showed him the end. The end was seen in the stars of the sky: "As many as these stars are so will your offspring be," said the Lord to him. Suddenly, Abraham was able to see the end. He was able to pass through the boundaries of space and time and look into the future and see his destiny, his purpose, and his calling. Are you able to see the end? Are you able to look through the skies of your calling and see the stars? If you want to be effective in your calling, you need to see the end. You need to ask yourself this question: "Lord when you call me home, what should I have achieved through my calling for your Kingdom?" He will show you. If your calling has no visions for the end then there is something lacking. Jesus said He knew where He came from and where He was going. Martin Luther King once said: *"I have a dream that one day on the red hills of Georgia the sons of former slaves and the sons of former slave owners will be able to sit down together at the table of brotherhood"* (Speech at the Civil Rights March in Washington, 28 August 1963). Dr. King saw the end in his dream. He visualized what would happen if he succeeded in his battle against unrighteousness and racial discrimination.

Moses did the same at the end of his life. In Deuteronomy 32:48–52 we read that God brought him up on Mt. Nebo in Moab and let him view the land of Canaan, the land that God had promised to the Israelites. Moses was called to lead his people to that land. Though he was supposed to bring them there, due to a lapse of faith, he could not do so personally. Now he is standing at the mountaintop and looking at the Promised Land. I imagine how much he looked with passion and excitement as his eyes traveled into the future and he sees the children of Israel playing on the hills of Canaan and the shepherds dwelling on the green fields and rivers. He fantasizes how one day cities will be established from the ground and the Jewish people will live in freedom in that land. Truly, he served the Lord and he saw the end. Now it was time for him to be with the Lord. It is in seeing the victorious end that we are able to hope and go through every challenge and every difficulty. We only have to see one thing: the victorious end! Just like what the apostle Paul said: *"Therefore we do not loose heart. Though outwardly we are wasting away, yet inwardly we are being renewed day by day"* (1 Corinthians 4:16). He said this because he saw the end. He saw the Gentiles and the Jews both worshipping the same Christ and receiving the same good news of the Gospel. At the end of his race he said: *"I have fought the good fight, I have finished the race, I have kept the faith. Now there is in store for me the crown of righteousness, which the Lord, the righteous judge, will award to me on that day — and not only to me but also to all who have longed for his appearing"* (2 Timothy 4:7–8).

9

CALLING IN PROCESS

This chapter emphasizes the continuity of our calling. To start, the calling is something, but to fulfill it is something else. As we walk in the pathways of our calling, we learn more about how to stand firm and fulfill our life's mission in God's Kingdom. Jesus Christ is the greatest example of someone who brought His calling into full completion. Jesus was born for the purpose of setting the captives free, proclaiming freedom to the prisoners, and healing the sick. Along the journey, He faced the Pharisees and the teachers of the law. However, the challenges from the religious establishment did not shake Him. He was wounded and bruised for our iniquities. He died on the cross for our sins and brought salvation to our lives. While dying on the cross He said: "It is finished." After three days, He rose again and conquered death. Now He is seated at the right hand of the Father and will return for the final battle. This, in short, was the calling of our Lord Jesus Christ.

What Can Stop you?

Challenges are always there. The more challenges we face, the stronger we become. You have to realize that you are continually in a battlefield; you are in the middle of a battle between God's Kingdom and Satan. This means that Satan will use all of his forces to stop you. The future of your calling is in the way you answer this question: **Who can stop me?** Jesus said many are called but few are chosen. Therefore, you need to answer this question very seriously! Who is able to stop you? Is it money, people, family situations, or life circumstances? What can stop you?

When Jesus started His ministry, He went to the desert and fasted for forty days. Satan challenged Him in many ways, but powerfully He rebuked Satan. He did not come out of the desert weary, tired, afraid, or weak. No! He came out as the victorious and powerful Son of God who was ready for every challenge!

Many people are out of the game when a little challenge comes their way. God is watching them. Remember God will never allow Satan to challenge you beyond your ability. Nothing should be able to stop you! Paul said: *"But whatever was to my profit I now consider loss for the sake of Christ. What is more, I consider everything a loss compared to the surpassing greatness of knowing Jesus Christ my Lord, for whose sake I have lost everything... . But one thing I do: Forgetting what is behind and straining toward what is ahead, I press on toward the goal to win the prize for which God has called me heavenward in Christ Jesus. All of us who are mature take such a view of things"* (Philippians 3:7–15).

Are you ready to consider everything a loss for the sake of Jesus Christ? Are you ready to face the challenge? Who or what is able to stop you? Make up your mind now!

Be Disciplined

The word "disciple" comes from the word "discipline." God is looking for disciplined soldiers and people who take their tasks seriously. The body of Christ lacks discipline. Discipline means being consistent. God is a businessman and we are His sons and daughters running His business. To run a business, you need discipline. One of the reasons why the body of Christ has not yet reached the world with the message of the Gospel is that we have not yet settled our priorities right. We are not yet dead to the flesh, and we are not disciplined yet! Why is it that every famous company such as General Motors, Samsung, and Coca Cola, to name a few, are able to reach the remotest areas of the world with their products? They have the discipline, that's why. They have people who passionately believe in the products they are making. Therefore, they work as hard as they can. They invest their time, they are trained constantly, and they are consistent!

Unfortunately, what do some Christians do? They are busy with their own social clubs. They are behind every sign and every wonder, forgetting that they have to be disciplined. They need to come out from the spiritual circus and carnivals and enter the real world and prove to the world the life-changing power of the Lord Jesus Christ. I hope you and I are not part of these types of circuses and carnival Christians! Discipline has the following elements that you need for your calling. Having discipline means you must:

- Sacrifice your time
- Sacrifice your energy
- Be consistent; work with prayer and have a strategy
- Have the word of honor
- Take every responsibility seriously

Do Not Complain

The apostle Paul said in Philippians 2:14: *"Do everything without complaining or arguing, so that you may become blameless and pure children of God, without fault in a crooked and depraved generation."* Many people live their lives complaining and arguing. They are almost never satisfied. They complain about everything and everybody. God doesn't accept the works of a complainer. God wants us to work out our calling with joy and peace.

Knowing Your Purpose: Shaking the Devil's Kingdom

In the beginning of this chapter, I dealt with the challenges we may receive in the path of fulfilling our calling. I asked you to answer this important question: "Who or what is able to stop you?" However, it is time for you to not only be challenged but also to be on the offensive. Challenge the devil and his forces. Here is a very important question: "What do you do in your life that challenges the devil?" What do you do that gives the devil and his servants restless hours? What do you do that will shake the devil's kingdom? The answer is, 'fulfill your purpose'! Knowing your calling is not enough; you must fulfill your purpose.

There is a difference between purpose and calling! Let me explain it this way: God called Jesus, His Son, to come into the world and die on the cross to save mankind from sin. This was His calling! If He refused to die, then His calling would not have been fulfilled! However, Jesus was not the only person who died on the cross; there were many before Him. Many died on the cross. This does not make them Messiahs! What was the difference between Jesus and those others who died on the cross? The difference lies in the purpose for dying on the cross. The purpose of Christ was different! The purpose of Jesus Christ was to redeem mankind from death. He fulfilled His calling: *"Having canceled the written code, with its regulations that was against us and that stood opposed to us; He took it away, nailing it to the cross. Having disarmed the powers and authorities, He made a public specta-cle of them triumphing over them by the cross"* (Colossians 2:14–15). That is why the apostle John says in 1 John 3:8: *"The reason (the purpose) the Son of God appeared was to destroy the devil's work."* Furthermore, 1 John 4:4 says: *"Greater is he who is in you than he who is in the world."* Who then is in you? Jesus Christ is in you! Because He lives in you, now His purpose becomes your purpose! His purpose was to destroy the power of the enemy! Therefore, what-ever your calling may be whether you are an artist, a doctor, a mother, a taxi driver, or a president of a nation, your purpose has to be the same as Christ's purpose — destroying the kingdom of Satan here on earth.

Everyday, the devil is controlling families; that is why there are so many divorces and children on drugs. We are the salt of the world. We must destroy the power of sin here on earth; we have to block the ways of Satan. How can we do this? By combining your calling with your purpose!

Jesus said: *"Go into all the world and preach the good news to all creation. Whoever believes and is baptized will be saved, but whoever does not believe will be condemned. And these signs will accompany those who believe: In my name they will drive out demons; they will speak in new tongues; they will pick up snakes with their hands; and when they drink deadly poison, it will not hurt them at all; they will place their hands on sick people, and they will get well"* (Mark 16:15–18).

Until today, you thought these things were the works of a preacher or a pastor. No! Jesus was speaking to the universal body of believers, and you are one of them. Use your authority! Look into your hands; you have received the power to achieve your purpose! You have the right to heal and to pray for the sick. You have the right to cast out devils, and you have the right to destroy the power of the enemy by proclaiming the Good News!

Telling the Good News is not confined to physical churches or the pulpit. It can be done in the marketplace, in the taxi, in the office, at home, in the factory and at schools. The world is sick. Heal the world in the Name of Jesus! Look at your city, your country, even your family. Imagine them being free from the bondage of Satan. What would happen? The world is dying without Christ. You are a minister regardless of who you are or how old you are! You belong to the Ministry of God's People. You can make a difference.

The Last Word

I pray that by reading this book you have entered into a new realm of experience. Wherever you are and whatever you do, you have to realize that you are made for a purpose, and you have a specifically designed calling in your life. That is the perfect will of God for you. Choosing this journey will be a blessing for you as the Lord gives you every possible tool to fulfill your calling. The work is many but the workers are few. Remember: *There is no unemployment in the Kingdom of God.* Close your eyes and imagine the glorious end! Imagine how many souls and nations will be blessed by you and through you. Indeed, you are very important!

Samuel Lee

ABOUT THE AUTHOR

Samuel Lee graduated from Leiden University with a degree in Sociology of Non-Western Societies. He also has a PhD in Sociology and a Habilitation from the University of Herisau. He specializes in cultural and religious sociology in Japan. His four years of habilitation research resulted in the book *Rediscovering Japan, Reintroducing Christendom: 2000 Years of Christian History in Japan* (University Press of America: Hamilton Books, 2010).

Samuel Lee is the founder and president of Jesus Christ Foundation Ministries and Samuel Lee World Evangelism, which reaches nations with the gospel of Jesus Christ. He has established churches and ministries in Cyprus, Ghana, Nigeria, and the Philippines. Samuel Lee World Evangelism offers tapes/videos/CDs and DVDs free of charge to all who reside in developing or underdeveloped nations. From prison cells in South Africa to schools in Ghana or churches in Japan, Korea, and the Philippines, Samuel Lee's ministry reaches more than 80 nations worldwide.

He is also the founder and president of Foundation University: Education Without Borders, which offers tuition-free academic/theological education for less-privileged migrants and citizens of the developing world. Foundation University is a private non-governmental institution and a member of the European Evangelical Accreditation Association.

Samuel Lee has worked to create and support programs for the rights of undocumented migrants in the Netherlands, and he has helped to establish organizations defending the rights of these migrants. He also won an African Roots Movement award in 2008 for his solidarity with the African community in Amsterdam.

He has often been a guest on television programs for *Family7*, a Dutch Christian Channel, as well as on the *Sid Roth Show* in the USA. He has been featured in various Christian newspapers in the Netherlands, such as *Nederlandse Dagblad* (October 6, 2007).

In November 2004, he was featured on the cover of *Ministries Today*, a magazine for Christian leaders in the USA.

He is the author of several books with the latest being released in early 2010, *Rediscovering Japan, Reintroducing Christendom: 2000 Years of Christian History in Japan* (University Press of America: Hamilton Books), and in February 2008, *Understanding Japan*

Through the Eyes of Christian Faith (iUniverse). His other recent titles include the following: *Journey with Paul: A Simplified Survey of the Pauline Books* (Foundation University Press), *Father — a Love Story Untold* (Xulon Press), *Blessed Migrants: A Biblical Perspective on Migration & What Every Migrant Needs to Know* (Foundation University Press). His autobiography is titled *Soldier of the Cross: The Amazing Story of a Muslim who met Christ* (Creation House).

Further, Samuel Lee with his book *Understanding Japan through the Eyes of Christian Faith* has helped train and inspire hundreds of missionaries to reach the Japanese people with the gospel of Jesus Christ.

He is a member of various Christian and scientific associations, such as the Association of Christian Sociologist, the Japan Sociological Society (University of Tokyo), the European Evangelical Accreditation Association, the Japan Evangelical Missionary Association, and many other institutions.

Samuel Lee and his wife Sarah live in Amsterdam and have three children.

About JCF Ministries

Jesus Christ Foundation Ministries is the group name for all the ministries and services offered by Dr. Samuel Lee. Jesus Christ Foundation Ministries consists of the following organizations:

✝ Jesus Christ Foundation Churches

✝ Jesus Christ Foundation Child Aid

✝ Samuel Lee World Evangelism

✝ Foundation University

✝ Foundation University Press

Dr. Samuel Lee's Websites

* *

✝ www.jcfchurch.com

✝ www.slwe.net

✝ www.foundationuniversity.com

✝ www.blessedmigrants.org

✝ www.projectjapan.org

✝ www.samlee.org (Personal Blog)

INVITE DR. SAMUEL LEE

To invite Samuel Lee to speak, please contact info@ slwe.net. Samuel Lee is available to give conferences or seminars on the following subjects:

✠ *Blessed Migrants Seminar* describes the role of migrants both in the Bible as well as in the current global context.

✠ *Anointed For Calling: Discover Your Calling & Transform the World* deals with questions such as "What is my calling?" and "For what has God anointed me in life?" Remember, there is no unemployment in the Kingdom of God!

✠ *Touch Me Not Satan* is a challenging seminar on spiritual warfare and the strategy for having a life full of victories. Various spiritual factors are discussed in this seminar, helping us to live our lives on the offensive frontlines.

✠ ***Understanding Japan*** is designed for those who are interested in Japan and have the vision to share the gospel with the Japanese people. Samuel Lee systematically explores various aspects of Japanese culture, society, and Church/Missiological history.

✠ ***Journey throughout the Old Testament*** is a one-week to ten-day seminar dealing with very important basics of the Old Testament.

✠ ***Apostle Paul*** is a one-week seminar dealing with very important aspects of the theology of the Apostle Paul.

✠ ***Church, Poverty, & Social Transformation*** is a two-day seminar on the role of the Church in society for advancing the Kingdom of God in order to bring forth social transformation in our nations. This seminar is created to encourage unity between various denominations as well as promote the establishment of indigenous Christianity and is specially designed for Christians from the developing world.

OTHER BOOKS BY SAMUEL LEE

- **_Blessed Migrants_** @14.95 U$/12.95 €

A Biblical Perspective on Migration & What Every Migrant Needs to Know

Also available in Audio Book @24.95 U$/19.95 € MP3 format @12.95 U$/9.95 €

- **_Soldier of the Cross_** @14.95 U$/12.95 €

The Amazing Story of a Muslim Man Who Met Christ

Also available in other languages: Italian, Korean, Japanese

- **_Father, A Love Story Untold_** @14.95 U$/12.95 €

The Heart of God the Father will be revealed to you in a special way

Also available in other languages: Korean, Farsi, & Tagalog

- ***Anointed for Calling*** @14.95 U$/12.95 €

Discover your calling and transform the world

Also available in other languages: French & Korean

- ***Understanding Japan Through the Eyes of Christian Faith*** @16.95 U$/14.95 €

A sociological handbook for every Christian who is interested in reaching the Japanese people with the gospel of Jesus Christ

- ***Journey with Paul*** @14.95 U$/12.95 €

A Simplified Survey of the Pauline Books

- ***Rediscovering Japan, Reintroducing Christendom*** @29.95 U$/24.95 €

2000 Years of Christian History in Japan

Audio Sermons

CD Series

- What Generosity Can Do? *3CD-Box,* 19.95 U$, 14.95 €
- Touch me Not Satan: *7CD-Box, 34.95 U$,* 19.95 €
- When You Go Through Trials: *3CD-Box,* 19.95 U$, 14.95 €
- Kingdom of Heaven: *3CD-Box,* 19.95 U$, 14.95 €
- You and God: *3CD-Box,* 19.95 U$, 14.95 €
- The Power of Vision: *2CD-Box,* 12.95 U$, 9.95 €

CD Single Title

- Samuel Lee's testimony — 7.95 U$, 5.95 €
- Expect a Miracle — 7.95 U$, 5.95 €
- Four corners of Faith — 7.95 U$, 5.95 €
- The True Pentecost — 7.95 U$, 5.95 €

- The Heart — 7.95 U$, 5.95 €
- How to Remain in your Calling — 7.95 U$, 5.95 €
- Justice and Grace — 7.95 U$, 5.95 €
- What Hope Can Do? — 7.95 U$, 5.95 €
- What Is So Special about Woman? — 7.95 U$, 5.95 €
- The God Factor — 7.95 U$, 5.95 €
- Manifesto of Grace — 7.95 U$, 5.95 €
- Power of Love — 7.95 U$, 5.95 €

DVD Series

- What Generosity Can Do? 3DVD-Box, 38.95 U$, 29.95 €
- Touch Me Not Satan: Spiritual Warfare Series. 7DVD-Box, 90.95 U$, 69.95 €
- Church: 4DVD-Box, 51.95 U$, 39.95 €
- When You Go Through Trials: 3DVD-Box, 38.95 U$, 29.95 €
- I Will Series: The Promises of God throughout the Bible. 3DVD-Box, 38.95 U$. 29.95 €
- I am "The Key to Success and Happiness": 2DVD-Box, 25.95U$, 19.95 €

DVD Single Titles

- Marriage — 12.95 U$, 9.95 €
- Relationship and Borders — 12.95 U$, 9.95 €

- Character Matters — 12.95 U$, 9.95 €
- Before anything, I am Human being — 12.95 U$, 9.95 €
- Biblical Rights of Migrants — 12.95 U$, 9.95 €

* Transportation Cost will be added to the price of total items order

To Order

Call Us: 0031-20-699 48 97 ~ 0031-20-4167308

Fax Us: 0031-20-4167309

Email Us: info@slwe.net

Visit Us: www.slwe.net